This book is a work of fiction. Any references to historical events, real people, or real places are used fictitiously. Other names, characters, places, and events are products of the author's imagination, and any resemblance to actual events or places or persons, living or dead, is entirely coincidental.

LITTLE SIMON
An imprint of Simon & Schuster Children's Publishing Division • 1230 Avenue of the Americas, New York, New York 10020 • First Little Simon hardcover edition June 2025 • © 2025 by Simon & Schuster, LLC. Also available in a Little Simon paperback edition. All rights reserved, including the right of reproduction in whole or in part in any form. LITTLE SIMON is a registered trademark of Simon & Schuster, LLC, and associated colophon is a trademark of Simon & Schuster, LLC. For information about special discounts for bulk purchases, please contact Simon & Schuster Special Sales at 1-866-506-1949 or business@simonandschuster.com. The Simon & Schuster Speakers Bureau can bring authors to your live event. For more information or to book an event contact the Simon & Schuster Speakers Bureau at 1-866-248-3049 or visit our website at www.simonspeakers.com. Series designed by Laura Roode. Book designed by Chani Yammer. The text of this book was set in Usherwood.
Manufactured in the United States of America 0425 LAK 10 9 8 7 6 5 4 3 2 1
Library of Congress Cataloging-in-Publication Data
Names: Green, Poppy, author. | Bell, Jennifer (Jennifer A.), 1977– illustrator. Title: Sunflower hour / by Poppy Green; illustrated by Jennifer A. Bell. Description: First Little Simon paperback edition. | New York: Little Simon, 2025. | Series: The adventures of Sophie Mouse; 22 | Audience term: Children | Summary: Sophie Mouse plans a picnic to celebrate the hour when the sunflowers are in best bloom, but no one seems to be interested. Identifiers: LCCN 2024040430 (print) | LCCN 2024040431 (ebook) | ISBN 9781665970549 (paperback) | ISBN 9781665970556 (hardcover) | ISBN 9781665970563 (ebook) Subjects: LCSH: Mice—Juvenile fiction. | Sunflowers—Juvenile fiction. | Parties—Juvenile fiction. | Summer—Juvenile fiction. | Animals—Juvenile fiction. | CYAC: Mice Fiction | Animals—Fiction. | Sunflowers—Fiction. | Parties—Fiction. | LCGFT: Animal fiction. Classification: LCC PZ7.G82616 St 2025 (print) | LCC PZ7.G82616 (ebook) | DDC [Fic]—dc23/eng/20250124
LC record available at https://lccn.loc.gov/2024040430
LC ebook record available at https://lccn.loc.gov/2024040431

the adventures of
SOPHIE MOUSE

22

Sunflower Hour

By Poppy Green • Illustrated by Jennifer A. Bell

LITTLE SIMON

New York Amsterdam/Antwerp London Toronto Sydney/Melbourne New Delhi

Contents

Chapter 1:
The Last Day of School
1

Chapter 2:
The Sunflower Hunt
13

Chapter 3:
A Brilliant Idea
23

Chapter 4:
Summer Plans
33

Chapter 5:
Countdown to Bloom Time
41

Chapter 6:
Bad Luck
51

Chapter 7:
The Shrinking Guest List
63

Chapter 8:
Party of One?
79

Chapter 9:
A Pop-Up Party
95

Chapter 10:
Golden Hour
107

Chapter 1

The Last Day of School

Sophie Mouse turned to gaze out the open window of the schoolhouse. Early afternoon sunbeams streamed in and spilled down onto her desk.

Mrs. Wise was reading aloud from the final pages of *An Alarmingly Large Strawberry in Tinytown*. It was a special treat for the last day of school.

Sophie sighed as she gazed outside. She loved read-aloud time. But today it was hard to follow along.

Summer vacation was just minutes away!

What would Sophie do with all her free time? She could paint every day! She could stop in at her mom's bakery to say hello. And to grab a treat, of course.

Most of all, Sophie hoped to explore. Maybe she would find a part of Silverlake Forest she had never seen before.

But was there anywhere she hadn't already discovered?

She had already explored Crystal Cave with her friends Hattie Frog and Owen Snake. They'd camped at Pine Crest Campground, too. One time they'd even found a hidden cottage deep in the woods.

Mrs. Wise shut the book loudly, and Sophie snapped out of her summer daydream.

The mystery of Tinytown's giant strawberry had been solved. But Sophie had missed the ending!

I'll have to borrow the book from the library and read it myself, she thought.

"Besides strawberries, what are some things you grow in your gardens?" Mrs. Wise asked the class.

"Lettuce!" called out James Rabbit.

"We grow all kinds of flowers," Piper chimed in.

That makes sense, thought Sophie. Piper was a hummingbird, and she loved flower nectar.

"Lovely!" said Mrs. Wise. "Does anyone have a favorite flower?"

Sophie raised her hand.

"Marigolds!" she declared. "No, daffodils. Or buttercups? Well, I like lilies, too."

The class giggled as Sophie held her head in her hands.

There were so many wonderful flowers. How could she choose just one?

"I like sunflowers," said Piper. "It's my mom's favorite too. Every summer she visits a sunflower field in the forest."

Sophie's ears perked up. A sunflower field? In the forest?

Just then Malcolm Mole pointed at the clock on the wall.

"It's two o'clock!" he shouted.

"So it is," Mrs. Wise said, chuckling. "School is dismissed. I will see you all again when we smell a hint of autumn in the air."

 Everyone jumped out of their seats. They hurried to their cubbies to pack up their things.

Sophie's little brother, Winston, was the first out the door.

"Summer vacation!" he shouted, pumping his fists in the air.

But Sophie hung back.

"Piper, where is that sunflower field?" Sophie asked.

Piper scratched her head.

"I can't remember exactly," she replied. "I've only been there once with my mom. But I do remember a big juniper tree. We rested our wings there. And there was a yummy berry bush nearby."

"Thanks!" Sophie said. She turned to catch up with Hattie and Owen.

Piper waved a wing. "Have a good summer!"

"I will!" replied Sophie. "Because I have a brand-new place to explore!"

Chapter 2

The Sunflower Hunt

Sophie caught up to Hattie and Owen as they headed out of the schoolyard.

"Come with us to Forget-Me-Not Lake!" Hattie said to Sophie.

Sophie stopped short.

"Can we go find that sunflower field first?" she pleaded. "Please?"

Hattie shrugged and looked at Owen.

Owen shrugged too. "Why not?" he said.

"Okay," said Hattie. "But then we go to the lake. It's so hot!"

Sophie led the way to the only big juniper tree she knew. The path took them through some dense woods, past Goldmoss Pond, but not as far as Hickory Hill.

Finally Sophie stopped at the base of a tall tree.

"A juniper!" Hattie exclaimed.

Sophie inhaled a deep breath. Sure enough, she could smell something sweet nearby.

"We're close," Sophie declared, her whiskers twitching.

Fifty paces on, they came to a mulberry bush. The branches were heavy with purple-black berries.

"This must be the berry bush Piper mentioned," Sophie said.

"Then the sunflowers must be around here . . . somewhere," Hattie said, looking around.

Owen slithered up into a tree for a better view. Hattie hopped farther down the path and circled back.

Sophie moved some branches aside and stepped through into a clearing atop a ledge.

But there were no sunflowers in sight. Had Sophie misunderstood Piper's directions?

Then Owen called out from overhead. "Look! Down there!"

Sophie inched forward and looked down, over the ledge. Then she gasped.

Just below, a field of tall green flower stalks seemed to stretch on forever!

Sophie had walked through this part of the forest so many times before. She just had never bothered to look down.

"The sunflowers are still buds," said Hattie.

"So the seeds aren't ready for snacking yet," added Owen. "Good thing these mulberries are here."

He used his tail to pop one into his mouth.

Sophie scrambled up onto a big rock to get a better look at Sunflower Field. *Oh, just imagine what they would look like in full bloom!*

Sophie wanted so badly to paint them. If only she could reach down and pick one. Then she could use ground-up petals in her pigment.

"Can we go to the lake now?" Owen asked.

"Fine, fine," Sophie answered, scampering down.

The sunflower bloom was still a few days away, at least.

But when it happened, Sophie wanted to be ready, paintbrush in hand!

A Brilliant Idea

Sophie, Hattie, and Owen got to Forget-Me-Not Lake while the sun was still beating down.

Hattie and Owen shrieked as they cannonballed into the water.

Sophie didn't like swimming as much as her friends did. But she loved floating on her raft, which Hattie and Owen had made just for her.

She paddled out into the middle of the lake, and her friends raced to get to her first.

Then Sophie lounged on her raft while Hattie hopped from one lily pad to another. Owen made ripples as he swam underwater.

Sophie's mind drifted back to Sunflower Field.

The whole field in bloom would be an amazing sight with all those happy yellow flowers waving in the breeze.

Maybe tomorrow she would get up early and bring her breakfast there. And lunch. And dinner. So many picnics at Sunflower Field, all summer long!

Then Sophie sat up straight on her raft.

"I have an amazing idea!" she shouted, jumping up onto her feet.

Unfortunately, the raft wasn't stable enough for that. It flew out from under Sophie.

She went down—*splash!*—into the lake.

"Sophie!" Owen and Hattie cried out. They swam toward their friend as fast as they could.

Luckily Sophie was wearing her seedpod vest. She bobbed effortlessly atop the water. Even her whiskers were barely wet!

"Are you okay?" Hattie asked as they pulled Sophie toward the shore.

"I'm better than okay!" Sophie replied. "I'm going to put on a sunflower party!"

Hattie and Owen's worried looks changed to puzzled looks.

"A what?" Hattie asked.

"A sunflower party," Sophie repeated. "When the sunflowers reach full bloom. Picture it: a picnic with food and decorations. And everyone can come see Sunflower Field at its best!"

"Oh," Owen said simply. "Well, do you want to get back on the raft?"

But Sophie shook her head. She towed her raft out of the water and tied it up to the reeds.

"I have a party to plan," Sophie declared. "There's not a moment to waste!"

Off she ran, leaving wet paw prints behind her all the way home.

Chapter 4

Summer Plans

By the time Sophie got home, her dad was pulling a potpie out of the oven. The smell of summer squash, potatoes, carrots, peas, and thyme filled their house.

It was Last Day of School Potpie—a Mr. Mouse specialty!

"Happy vacation!" Sophie's dad announced.

Sophie hurried upstairs to change into dry clothes. She still managed to beat Winston to the table.

As soon as they began eating, Sophie started telling her family about her after-school adventure.

"Sunflower Field?" her mom said. "Past Goldmoss Pond?"

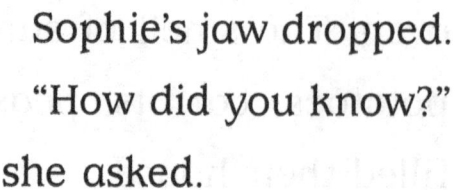

Sophie's jaw dropped. "How did you know?" she asked.

"I go every year after the flowers finish blooming," Mrs. Mouse explained.

"A little shake on the stalks, and all the sunflower seeds rain down into my baskets!"

Sophie had seen those jars of seeds lined up at her mom's bakery. So *that's* where they all came from.

Oooh! Maybe she could use some sunflower seeds to make yummy treats for the party!

Sophie opened her mouth to ask her mom. But Winston started talking about his day.

"I went with James to fly his kite. Well, I mostly *watched* James fly his kite." Winston frowned. "I wish *I* had a kite."

Sophie swallowed a mouthful of potpie. "I have a kite somewhere," she said. "You can have it."

"Really, Sophie?" Winston replied. "Thanks!"

After dinner Sophie went up to her bedroom and peered under her bed.

There! Her old kite was stuffed all the way in the back. She grabbed the kite's string and out it came, tangled up and coated with dust.

Achoo! Sophie sneezed.

Then her eyes fell on the big hole in the middle of the kite. Suddenly, she remembered the last time she had flown it. The kite had snagged on a rosebush.

Sophie brought the kite downstairs anyway.

"Sorry, Winston," she said. "I don't think this is going to fly."

Winston crossed his arms and pouted.

But then George Mouse took the kite from Sophie.

"It might not fly right now," he said. "But it's nothing we can't repair."

Winston jumped up from his chair. "Really? I'll get my toolbox now!"

"When you're done, I'll paint something on it for you," Sophie offered. "Maybe a big sunflower?"

Winston ran off, hugging the kite to his chest.

"Maybe!" he called back.

Countdown to Bloom Time

All week long, Sophie rushed through her morning chores. She made her bed. She swept the floors as fast as she could. She took in the clean laundry and put her clothes away.

Then Sophie would grab her sketchbook and paint box. She would run past Winston, hard at work on his kite, and burst out of the house.

It was a long way to Sunflower Field. Even so, Sophie would skip the whole way—down the long path into town, past the town hall and the bookstore.

She always stopped in at her mom's bakery and got a muffin to go. Then she would skip on toward Sunflower Field.

Each day Sophie would scramble up onto the big rock. And each day the sunflower buds looked a little bit bigger.

Sophie never got tired of painting the sunflowers.

She would try to match the colors of the petals, but they kept changing. As buds, the petals were more greenish-yellow. As they unfurled, the yellow became more golden.

When Sophie wasn't painting, she was working on decorations for the party. She gathered pine cones and strung them together with ribbon.

Sophie also worked on making invitations. She made one for her parents, one for Winston, one for Hattie, and one for Owen.

And of course, she made one for Piper and her family, too.

Sophie kept the invitations tied up in a bundle in her  satchel. When it seemed like it was peak bloom time, she would hand them out to her guests.

One hot afternoon, Sophie came up with a plan to make picnic blankets for the party. She needed some reeds, so she made her way to Forget-Me-Not Lake.

By the time Sophie got there, the tops of her ears were hot to the touch.

Hattie and Owen were playing in the water.

"Sophie!" Owen waved and called out to her. "Where have you been? We've been going by your house every day looking for you."

"Come in!" Hattie added. "The water is perfect!"

But Sophie was too busy to play with her friends. Instead she sat down in the shade of the reeds.

One by one, Sophie picked and braided reeds into picnic blankets, all through the heat of the day.

Bad Luck

A few days later Sophie arrived at Sunflower Field and squeaked with delight.

The sunflowers had grown so much overnight! Just yesterday their centers had been light green. Now they were brown.

The flowers were nearly in full bloom!

It was finally time to hand out the party invitations.

"See you tomorrow, sunflowers!" Sophie called out. "I'll be back with friends!"

Then she bounded away. Her satchel, heavy with invitations, bounced against her hip.

Her first stop was Piper's house. Sophie called up from the ground below, and Piper zipped down.

"Can you come to my party tomorrow?" Sophie asked, pulling out an invitation.

"Actually, tomorrow is my mom's birthday," Piper replied. "We've already planned a lunch to celebrate."

Sophie's heart fell. She would never have discovered Sunflower Field if it hadn't been for Piper and her mom. Sophie really wanted them both to be there.

But she couldn't argue with a birthday party.

"That's okay, then," Sophie said. "Tell your mom happy birthday."

How unlucky, thought Sophie as she walked toward town. *Two parties on the same day.*

Sophie walked into town and entered her mom's bakery.

"Mom!" she called out in a sing-song voice. "Here's your invitation!"

But Mrs. Mouse didn't look up. She was whisking a bowl of frosting while peering inside the oven. Then she put the bowl down on the table and started kneading dough.

Sophie moved closer.

"Oh!" her mom said. She jumped, noticing Sophie for the first time. "I didn't hear you come in."

Sophie tried again.

"I'm having the sunflower party tomorrow!" she announced. "Can we bake sunflower treats for it?"

Sophie's mom brushed her hands on her apron. Then she looked around at the mess of pots, pans, and baking sheets.

"Sweetheart, I have a mountain of things to make," she told Sophie. "I got a big order for Piper's mom's birthday tomorrow."

Sophie groaned. How much more bad luck could she get? Her mom was so busy making food for the other party that she couldn't help with Sophie's!

Unless . . .

"I'll help you," Sophie suggested. With teamwork, they could finish the birthday party order in no time at all.

Mrs. Mouse frosted a cake while Sophie started putting together tea sandwiches.

Then Sophie mixed muffin batter while her mom filled fruit tarts.

But even after all that work, they still had three kinds of cookies to make. Plus dozens of doughnuts, all for Piper's mom's party!

When would there be time to make Sophie's treats?

The Shrinking Guest List

The sun was starting to get lower in the sky, but Sophie and her mom were still working.

Sophie still needed to deliver Hattie's and Owen's invitations. So she left the bakery and ran out to find her friends.

She had a feeling she knew where to find them.

Sure enough, her friends were playing a game of swim tag at Forget-Me-Not Lake.

"Sophie! We've both missed you!" Hattie cried.

"You can be 'it!'" Owen added.

But once again, Sophie was all business, with no time for play.

"Tomorrow is the big day!" Sophie said to her friends. "The party! It's tomorrow!"

"The party?" Hattie repeated. She looked at Owen, confused.

"What party?" Owen asked.

Sophie was stunned. Did they really not remember?

The whole idea had come to her right here at the lake! Hattie and Owen had been the very first ones to know about it.

"The sunflower party, of course," Sophie said.

Hattie and Owen dragged themselves out of the water.

"We already saw the sunflowers with you," Hattie pointed out.

"Not in full bloom," Sophie protested. "They look magical. You have to see!"

She held out two invitations. Hattie and Owen reached out to take them.

But at the last moment, Sophie pulled them back. Her friends were still dripping wet, and Sophie had worked so hard to make the invitations. She didn't want them to get ruined.

"Hmm," Owen said. "If we go to your picnic, will you come play with us after?"

Sophie felt a lump rising in her throat. She blinked, trying to fight back tears.

Her friends didn't seem excited about the sunflowers. At all! Why hadn't they said yes to her invitation right away?

Bubbling over with anger and disappointment, Sophie tossed the invitations onto the rock. Then she ran off toward home.

As Sophie came up to her house, one thought made her feel a little better: *At least Winston and Dad will come tomorrow.*

Her mom was still working at the bakery, so Sophie, Winston, and Mr. Mouse had an early dinner together.

Winston was in a great mood.

"Dad helped me fix my kite today, but there wasn't enough wind to try it out." Winston crinkled his nose. "My whiskers tell me the weather tomorrow will be perfect!"

"Maybe out on Hickory Hill," Sophie's dad suggested.

Sophie pulled out her invitations.

"What about my party?" she said. "You can always fly your kite another day."

"But I've worked so hard on my kite!" Winston shouted.

"Now, let's remember our table manners," Mr. Mouse said calmly. "Sophie, please put the invitations away. Just until after dinner."

Sophie did as she was asked. But after dinner she huffed up to her bedroom and flopped down onto her bed.

Why didn't *anyone* want to come to her sunflower party?

Chapter 8

Party of One?

The next morning Sophie was up and out of the house before anyone else.

She had so much to carry to Sunflower Field. All the pine-cone vines she'd made were slung over one shoulder. Her paint box, easel, and canvas were tucked under her arm. With the other hand she clutched her lunch box.

Sophie had to stop to rest a few times along the way. But she was going to make the party happen . . . even if she was the only one there.

When she arrived, Sophie dropped her things by the juniper tree.

Then she hurried to the ledge and gasped.

A sea of brilliant yellow stretched out before her. The big, round flower heads pointed up toward the sky like they were soaking in the sunshine.

It was the most cheerful sight Sophie had ever seen! She couldn't help but smile.

If only her friends and family could see it too.

Sophie hung all her decorations.

Then she scrambled up onto the big rock and started eating her chickpea salad sandwich.

It was no sunflower treat feast. But it would have to do.

After eating, it was time to set up her painting easel.

She had made a vibrant shade of yellow paint from the daylilies growing behind her house.

With enough layers of paint, she hoped the yellow would match the brightness of the sunflowers.

At first Sophie thought very hard about each step. But before long she lost herself in brushstroke after brushstroke.

So many flowers. So many petals. In the background they all merged together into one.

When the canvas was covered with blooms, Sophie stepped back.

Not bad, she thought. It really did look like the flowers stretched on forever.

And yet the painting didn't feel finished. Something was missing.

At that moment Sophie heard a rustling in the woods behind her. There were twigs snapping and faraway footsteps. Lots of footsteps!

Sophie heard voices talking and laughing.

She turned to peer into the trees.

Coming up the path was a large group, led by Owen and Hattie. Winston was next, carrying his kite. Then came Sophie's mom and dad, their arms full with picnic baskets.

Over their heads, Piper and her hummingbird family circled the group. And there were even more birds and critters trailing behind.

"What—? Why—?" Sophie was so stunned, she could barely get out a word!

Piper landed on the ledge next to Sophie.

"My mom discovered your party invitation on our table this morning," Piper explained.

"I thought a sunflower party was such a lovely idea," Piper's mom added, landing on Sophie's other side. "I had to move my birthday lunch here!"

So they had packed up all the food and rounded up all the party guests . . . to join Sophie!

Sophie beamed at the crowd as they all gazed out at Sunflower Field.

It was time for the party to truly begin!

Chapter 9

A Pop-Up Party

Sophie helped her parents unpack the food: muffins, cookies, and the tea sandwiches she had helped her mom make. There were also veggie wraps, pasta salad, and watermelon slices.

Mrs. Mouse had even stayed up late to make sunflower-seed breadsticks and cookies frosted to look like sunflowers. Just for Sophie!

Sophie happily nibbled on food. Then she spotted Winston struggling with his kite. He was trying to catch a breeze.

"Here, I'll help you launch it," she told her brother.

A soft, sweet breeze kicked up. It carried the scent of the mulberries and made waves across the yellow sea of flower petals.

When the breeze reached them, Sophie called out, "Now!"

Winston took off running, pulling on the string. Sophie gave the kite a toss up into the air. It took off, high into the sky!

Everyone clapped and cheered.

Winston even let Sophie take a turn holding the string.

Then Winston asked, "Would you paint a big sunflower on my kite after all?"

"Of course," Sophie said, giving her brother a hug.

Later, Sophie, Owen, and Hattie climbed onto the big rock to get a better view of the field.

"You're right," Hattie said to Sophie. "The sunflowers looked nice as buds. But they look amazing in full bloom."

"Yeah," Owen agreed. "But do we still have to wait to pick the seeds?"

Oh! That reminded Sophie of something she had been wondering. She hurried over to her mom.

"How do you climb down the ledge every year?" Sophie asked. "To gather the sunflower seeds?"

Mrs. Mouse motioned for Sophie and her friends to follow. She led them farther down the path away from the juniper tree.

Soon they came to the top of a dried-up waterfall. Rocks of all sizes formed a rough-and-tumble stairway that led all the way down to the field.

Sophie, Hattie, and Owen climbed down slowly. When they reached the bottom, they looked up—and gasped in wonder.

The sunflowers stood so tall, they might have been trees. They nearly blocked out the whole sky!

"Wow," whispered Sophie. The sunflowers were awe-inspiring, no matter how you looked at them.

"Oooh, look!" Owen cried. A few sunflower seeds had already fallen to the ground.

Owen scooped them up. On the climb back up to the ledge, they cracked the seeds open on a rock.

Sophie nibbled a tender, nutty seed.

Mmmm. There was nothing like sunflower seeds fresh from the shell.

Golden Hour

The sun climbed higher in the sky, bathing the sunflowers in a golden light.

Now, thought Sophie, *sunflowers can't get any more beautiful than they are now!*

Sophie snuck away from the party to add a few more touches to her painting.

When she was done, Sophie linked one arm with Hattie's and put the other around Owen.

"I'm really happy you made it to the party," she told them. "I thought you didn't want to come."

Hattie and Owen looked at each other.

"We're sorry we didn't say yes right away," Hattie said.

"We know now the sunflowers are very important to you," Owen added.

Sophie looked down and kicked at a stone.

"I'd like to play at the lake tomorrow," she said, "if you'll both be there too."

"Yes!" Hattie and Owen said, beaming.

Soon it was time for Mrs. Hummingbird's birthday cake.

Piper put candles into the layer cake that Sophie and her mom had baked. Then they all sang "Happy Birthday."

Piper gave her mom a necklace made from bluestem grass and deep-red currants. Mr. Hummingbird gave her a book she'd been wanting.

"Thank you," Mrs. Hummingbird said. "This is the best birthday ever!"

Sophie cleared her throat.

"Um, actually, there's one more present," she said. She pulled out her canvas from behind her back.

"How beautiful!" Mrs. Hummingbird cried in delight as she looked over every detail of the painting.

Sophie had added Piper and her family hovering above the sunflowers. Off to one side was Winston, flying his kite. And on the other side were Hattie and Owen and Sophie, helping themselves to treats.

Family and friends together to celebrate sunflower hour. That was what her painting had been missing!

"It's amazing," Mrs. Hummingbird said. She gave Sophie a very big hug. "Thank you! I'm so happy to know someone loves these flowers as much as I do."

As they packed up their things to go home, Sophie felt sad that the sunflowers would fade in just a few weeks.

But then again, that was what made this time in full bloom so special.

Already, Sophie couldn't wait for next summer when the sunflowers would be in full bloom again.

She had a feeling that next year's sunflower party would be even bigger and better!

The End

the adventures of SOPHiE MOUSE

For excerpts, activities, and more about these adorable tales & tails, visit AdventuresofSophieMouse.com!

If you like Sophie Mouse, you'll love

the CRITTER club